Big Pig
and
Little Pig

Big Pig
and Little Pig

David McPhail

Green Light Readers
Harcourt, Inc.
Orlando   Austin   New York   San Diego   London

"I am hot," said Big Pig.

"Me, too," said Little Pig.

"I am going to make a pool,"
said Big Pig.

"Me, too," said Little Pig.

"I am going to dig a hole,"
said Big Pig.

"Me, too," said Little Pig.

"I am going to get a bucket,"
said Big Pig.

"Me, too," said Little Pig.

"I am going to fill up the pool,"
said Big Pig.

"Me, too," said Little Pig.

"Now I can sit back down," said Big Pig.

"Me, too!" said Little Pig.

Let's Dig In!

Make Big Pig's favorite snack.

WHAT YOU'LL NEED

bread

big cookie cutter
little cookie cutter

jam

knife

raisins

1 Cut a big circle and a little circle in your bread with the cookie cutters.

2 Spread jam on the big circle.

3 Cut one of the little circles in half. You'll use them for ears.

4 Make a pig face. Use raisins for the eyes and nostrils.

Write a sentence about your favorite snack. Share your sentence and your snack with a friend!

Meet the Author-Illustrator

David McPhail loves to draw pigs. When he
was a child, his favorite character was the pig
in the book *Charlotte's Web*. "Pigs tickle me,"
he says. "They're fun because they do such
silly things!" He hopes you giggled when you
read *Big Pig and Little Pig*!

For information about permission to reproduce
selections from this book,please write to Permissions,
Houghton Mifflin Harcourt Publishing Company
215 Park Avenue South, NY NY 10003.

www.hmhco.com

First Green Light Readers edition 2001
Green Light Readers is a trademark of Harcourt, Inc., registered in the
United States of America and/or other jurisdictions.

The Library of Congress has cataloged an earlier edition as follows:
McPhail, David M.
Big Pig and Little Pig/by David McPhail.
p. cm.
"Green Light Readers."
Summary: Although they like different things, Big Pig and
Little Pig enjoy spending time together.
[I. Pigs—Fiction. 2. Friendship—Fiction.] I. Title. II. Green Light reader.
PZ7.M2427Bi 2001
[E]—dc21   00-9725
ISBN 978-0-15-204818-1
ISBN 978-0-15-204857-0 (pb)

SCP 18 17 16 15 14 13
4500516544

Ages 4-6
Grades: K-1
Guided Reading Level: B-D
Reading Recovery Level: 4-5

Green Light Readers
For the reader who's ready to GO!

"A must-have for any family with a beginning reader."—*Boston Sunday Herald*

"You can't go wrong with adding several copies of these terrific books to your beginning-to-read collection."—*School Library Journal*

"A winner for the beginner."—*Booklist*

Five Tips to Help Your Child Become a Great Reader

1. Get involved. Reading aloud to and with your child is just as important as encouraging your child to read independently.

2. Be curious. Ask questions about what your child is reading.

3. Make reading fun. Allow your child to pick books on subjects that interest her or him.

4. Words are everywhere—not just in books. Practice reading signs, packages, and cereal boxes with your child.

5. Set a good example. Make sure your child sees YOU reading.

Why Green Light Readers Is the Best Series for Your New Reader

- Created exclusively for beginning readers by some of the biggest and brightest names in children's books

- Reinforces the reading skills your child is learning in school

- Encourages children to read—and finish—books by themselves

- Offers extra enrichment through fun, age-appropriate activities unique to each story

- Incorporates characteristics of the Reading Recovery program used by educators

- Developed with Harcourt School Publishers and credentialed educational consultants